Puss in Boots

Written by Anna Wilson

Illustrated by Denis Martynets

Collins

As the old miller lay dying, he called his son, Sam, to him.

"I wish I had lots of money to leave you," he said, "but you know how poor we are."

"Don't worry, Father," Sam said.

"Take my cat," the old miller said. "He's good at catching mice. Trust him – he'll make your fortune."

Sam wept. "What use is a cat? I can't sell it. I can't even eat it!"

"I hope not!" said the cat, appearing by his side. "If you ate me I wouldn't be able to help you."

"You? Help me?" said Sam. "But you're only a cat."

"Charming!" said the cat. "Give me a bag and a pair of boots and take me with you," he said. "You'll soon see what use I can be."

Sam shrugged. "All right," he said.

He found some boots and a bag and gave them to the cat.

"Are you hungry?" asked the cat.

"Oh yes," said Sam.

"Watch," said the cat.

He took the bag and went out into the fields, picked some fresh green leaves and put them into the bag.

Then he placed it near a rabbit hole, lay down next to it and pretended that he was fast asleep.

Soon, some rabbits came sniffing …

Quick as a flash, the cat leapt up and pulled the bag shut! The rabbits wriggled, but they were trapped.

"Your supper," said the cat, handing over the bag.

Sam was amazed. "You clever cat!"

The cat bowed low. "I have a plan. Leave one of the rabbits in the bag. We're going to give it to the king."

"Why?" Sam asked.

"You want to be rich, don't you?" said the cat.

"I do," said Sam, "but how will your plan make me rich?"

"Trust me," said the cat.

The cat went to the king. "Your Majesty," he said, bowing low. "I've brought you a present from my master, Lord Carabas."

"Please tell Lord Carabas that I'm delighted," said the king.

The cat went back to Sam and repeated what the king had said.

"But I'm not Lord Carabas," said Sam. "I'm a poor young man."

The cat winked. "Trust me," he said, "and your fortunes will change."

The next day, the cat put some grain into the bag before lying down and pretending to sleep.

This time, some partridges ran into it and were trapped.

"Here's your supper, master," said the cat. "Save one bird as before and I'll take it to the king."

The king was again very pleased.

The cat caught something different every day for the next two months. Every day his master had fresh food to eat and every day the king had a new gift from the mysterious Lord Carabas.

Soon the king grew curious. "I would like to meet Lord Carabas," he told the cat.

The cat knew that the king and his daughter travelled in their carriage every day, so he hatched a plan.

One day, Sam and the cat were walking by the river, near the king's palace.

They heard horses and carriages approaching.

"It's the king with his daughter, the beautiful Princess Grace!" cried the cat. "Quick, take off your jacket and don't say a word!"

"What on earth are you talking about?" Sam said, confused.

"Trust me," said the cat, "and you'll see."

Sam shrugged. "All right," he said.

He took off his jacket and waited.

As soon as the king's carriages appeared, the cat gave the miller's son a push.

SPLASH! He landed in the river!

The cat began to shout, "Help! My master, the Lord Carabas, is drowning. Help!"

The king saw Sam, splashing and gasping. "Save that man!" he shouted. "It's Lord Carabas! We must help him!"

The servants jumped into the river and pulled Sam out.

The poor young man was shivering, so blankets were fetched from the king's luggage.

"What happened?" the king asked.

"Robbers came, Your Majesty," said the cat. "They attacked my Lord Carabas and stole his jacket, his jewels and his money, then threw him in the river."

In fact, the clever cat had hidden the jacket behind a bush.

"Give Lord Carabas everything he needs," the king said to his servants.

The servants brought out fine clothes and jewels and gave them to Sam.

The king offered Sam and the cat a seat in his carriage. "You shall be my guests."

The miller's son looked very handsome in the king's clothes.

The king was pleased. "I know you're a generous man, Lord Carabas, but now I can see you're very handsome, too. Come and sit next to my daughter."

The cat winked at Sam.

Sam smiled at Princess Grace and she smiled too.

"Excuse me," said the cat, "I've got some jobs to do. I'll be back soon."

The clever cat had another plan.

He jumped down from the carriage and ran until he came to some men working in a field.

"The king is coming!" he cried "When he rides by, can you tell him that all the fields around here belong to my master, the Lord Carabas?"

The men shrugged. "All right," they said. It made no difference to them. They still got paid at the end of the day.

When at last the carriage came by, the king looked out at the lush crops. His fields were not nearly this plentiful and he called out, "Whose field is this?"

"Lord Carabas owns it!" said the men. "He owns all the fields around here," they added, grinning.

"So," the king said, turning to Sam. "You're generous, handsome *and* rich."

The cat watched from the field as his master smiled at Princess Grace and she smiled back.

"Excuse me," said the cat, "I have one more job to do. I'll see you soon!"

He knew of a castle, which sat on the road ahead.
It was owned by a terrible ogre.

Everyone was frightened of the ogre. Everyone except
the cat, of course. He bounded off, leaving the carriage
behind him, and soon arrived at the drawbridge.

"Hello," the cat shouted to the ogre.
"I've heard you can change into any kind
of creature you like. Is this true?"

"It is," the ogre replied.

"I don't believe you," said the cat.

The ogre roared, "You cheeky cat!"

Immediately he transformed into a lion, with a roar that was more terrifying than before.

The cat leapt out of the way.

The lion turned back into the ogre.

"See?" growled the ogre.

"'That was amazing!" the cat said. "I bet you can't turn into a smaller animal."

The ogre roared again. "I can turn into anything! Name any animal you like."

The cat said, "What about a mouse?"

The ogre laughed. "Easy! Watch …"

ZAP! The huge, ugly ogre turned into a tiny grey mouse.

The cat pounced on the mouse. "Got you!" he cried and he gobbled it up.

"A bit crunchy," he said with a grimace. "Never mind, now I must get ready for the king."

The cat found the ogre's servants. "We need a banquet for His Majesty!" he ordered. "The king is bringing his beautiful daughter and an important guest – Lord Carabas. The ogre wants everything to be perfect."

The servants were terrified of the ogre. So they worked as hard and as fast as they could.

The table was laid with delicious things. The castle was looking fabulous.

"Just in time!" cried the cat.

He ran to greet the king. "Welcome, Your Majesty, to the castle of Lord Carabas!"

The king was very impressed, "So," he said to Sam, "you're generous, handsome, rich *and* you have a magnificent castle."

Sam smiled and the princess smiled back.

"Dinner is served," said the cat, as he led the way over the drawbridge.

"Lord Carabas," said the king, "why don't you sit with my daughter?"

"Thank you, Your Majesty," said Sam.

The king and his party enjoyed a wonderful feast in the ogre's castle. They were waited on by the ogre's servants, who were too frightened to ask the cat what had happened to their master.

Sam and the princess looked into each other's eyes. They held hands and talked and talked. They couldn't get enough of each other's company.

At the end of the evening, the king raised a glass.

"To our host, Lord Carabas!" he said. "My Lord, is there anything I can do to repay you?"

"Well," said Sam. "I was wondering … can I marry your daughter?"

The king turned to the princess. "What do you think, my dear?" he asked.

"Yes!" she said.

So that's how the miller's son became the richest man in the land, married to the daughter of the king.

"I told you to trust me," said the cat.

"You did," said Sam, "and as a reward, I name you Lord Puss in Boots. You may have whatever you like to eat and you'll never have to catch a mouse ever again."

The cat smiled.

Not unless it's an ogre in disguise, he thought.

The nine lives of Puss in Boots

1 Puss

2 Hunter cat

4 Actor cat

3 Servant cat

5 Clever cat

6 Brave cat

7 Cunning cat

8 Party cat

9 Lord Puss in Boots

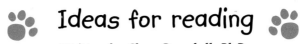
Ideas for reading
Written by Clare Dowdall, PhD
Lecturer and Primary Literacy Consultant

Reading objectives:
- increase familiarity with a wide range of books including fairy stories and retell orally
- identify themes and conventions
- make predictions from details stated and applied

Spoken language objectives:
- use spoken language to develop understanding through speculating, hypothesising, imagining and exploring ideas

Curriculum links: Geographical skills

Resources: pencil and paper for sketching, ICT for designing an advert

Build a context for reading
- Hand out the books and look at the picture on the front cover. Ask children to describe what they can see. Challenge them for interesting adjectives to describe Puss, e.g. cheeky, cunning.
- Discuss what the children already know about the traditional tale *Puss in Boots*. Can they name any characters and recount any events from the story?
- Read the blurb together and focus on the word "useful". Ask children to name some "useful" human qualities. Challenge them to predict how Puss might be "useful" in this story.

Understand and apply reading strategies
- Read pp2–3 aloud. Ask children to make a picture in their mind of what is happening at the beginning of the story, to deepen their understanding.
- Reread the line "Trust him – he'll make your fortune" to the group. Discuss what this means. Check that children understand what a "fortune" is.